DISCARD

FROM CAGE TO FREEDOM

FROM CAGE TO FREEDOM

A NEW BEGINNING FOR LABORATORY CHIMPANZEES

ILLUSTRATED WITH PHOTOGRAPHS

Linda Koebner

E. P. DUTTON   NEW YORK

LIBRARY OF CONGRESS CATALOGING IN PUBLICATION DATA
Koebner, Linda.
    From cage to freedom.
    Bibliography: p.
    Summary: The author relates her experiences in returning a group of laboratory chimpanzees to freedom in an animal preserve in Florida.
    1. Chimpanzees—Juvenile literature.   2. Chimpanzees as laboratory animals—Juvenile literature.   3. Lion Country Safari (Animal park: West Palm Beach, Fla.)—Juvenile literature. [1. Chimpanzees.   2. Chimpanzees as laboratory animals.   3. Lion Country Safari (Animal park: West Palm Beach, Fla.)   4. Wildlife conservation] I. Title.
QL795.C57K63   1981   639.9'79884409759   81-9834
ISBN 0-525-66755-5   AACR2

Published in the United States by Elsevier-Dutton Publishing Co., Inc., 2 Park Avenue, New York, N.Y. 10016. Published simultaneously in Canada by Clarke, Irwin & Company Limited, Toronto and Vancouver
DESIGNER: TRISH PARCELL
Printed in the U.S.A.   First edition

10   9   8   7   6   5   4   3   2   1

TO LARRY, JANET, ALVIN, SPARK,
NOLAN, COOPER, DOLL, AND SWING,
WHO GAVE ME THE GREATEST GIFT:
TRUST. AND TO ALL THE OTHER
CHIMPS I HAD TO LEAVE BEHIND.

CONTENTS

The following photographers have contributed their work to this book:

Bill Martin—pages 37, 57, 59, 75, 84, 106, 111.

Michael Miller—pages 10, 12, 17.

Tony Pfeiffer—pages 3, 5, 20, 22, 23, 24, 25, 26, 28, 45, 49, 55, 56, 58, 80 *(bottom)*, 82, 86, 87, 89, 92, 102.

Ken Rice—pages x, 9, 44.

The remaining photos were taken by the author, namely: Pages ii, 4, 27, 34, 39, 41, 46, 47, 48, 53, 54, 60, 63, 67, 70, 73, 76, 77, 80 *(top)*, 93, 94, 98, 100, 101, 103, 108.

ACKNOWLEDGMENTS

There are so many animals, human and nonhuman, who made it possible for me to share those special years with the chimps that it is not possible to mention them all. But special thanks must go to Dr. Art Kling of Rutgers University, who supplied the chance; to Dr. Moor-Jankowski of L.E.M.S.I.P., who allowed me the chance; and to all the people at Lion Country Safari, West Palm Beach, who gave me the chance.

I do want to thank especially: Bill Martin, who got us going and saw us through some rough times; Dr. Cecil Sutton, without whose expertise Doll, Nolan, and Spark might not have been around to write about; Patti Forkan, my special friend, who does not wear sneakers but who believed in us and knew how to let others know; Linda Marchant, who shared more than chimps with me; Tony Pfeiffer, who had the same dream; Rocky White and Mark Cussano, who really know chimps; Hans, who was always there; and my mother, who may not have realized what she began by introducing me to Bruno, but who loves me enough to understand.

And I thank every technician, warden, and fruit-stand owner who gave time, expertise, or bananas.

1 Beginnings

People always reacted with surprise when they first saw Bruno. To me, Bruno was a good friend; I accepted him just as he was and tended to forget that even I had done a double take the first time I saw him. Still, I have to admit there were some advantages to his appearance—like the day he saved me some money.

I was a senior in high school, working on a special project at Columbia University in New York City. I was driving my friend Bruno back to the university when we came to a tollbooth. I stopped and held out some change. The toll collector reached out, in an absentminded fashion, to take my money. Then he saw Bruno. His eyes widened, and he jerked his hand back into the booth.

"Move on, Lady. Get going," he choked out.

I pointed out that I had not yet paid.

"Just move along. Go on. Beat it."

People in New York are not prepared to see an uncaged chimpanzee.

Although Bruno was less than two years old and quite adorable, he was as strong as I was. He was also very intelligent and quick to learn. I was one of several people involved in teaching Bruno American Sign Language.

1

Chimpanzees are unable to make the same sounds people make. Yet they are able to use their hands well and to imitate human beings. A few years before, in Nevada, a chimp named Washoe had learned this language used by the deaf. Washoe could use it to communicate with human beings. We wanted Bruno to learn it too.

Chimpanzees are very special animals. They have amazed and amused humankind for hundreds of years. They seem to come as close as any nonhuman animal can to being a human being. Of the primates classified as great apes (gorilla, orangutan, chimpanzee), the chimpanzee looks the most like a human. Chimps' organs and body chemistry, even their blood types, are so similar to ours that in many cases they are even interchangeable with human organs and blood types.

We use chimpanzees in ways we don't ordinarily use a pet or a farm animal. Their intelligence and natural physical strength and flexibility enable them to do amazing circus acts. Their similarities to humans made them ideal for scientists to use them in the space program during the 1960's. Today medical researchers use them in experiments that are always frightening and often painful.

Ironically, the same animal who has been proved to be intelligent enough to use American Sign Language to communicate with humans is often taken from his mother when he is just a baby and greatly in need of her care and comfort, then put in the solitary confinement of a laboratory cage, where all too often boredom and loneliness cause him to die or to go mad.

When the chimpanzee is in his natural surroundings, in Africa, his family and community structure are similar to the way many humans still live today. Banding in groups of fifteen to twenty, the chimpanzees travel through their

CHIMPS PLAYING AND LAUGHING

territory, usually an area of about thirty square miles. They eat mainly fruits, vegetation, insects, and on occasion some meat. Most of the day is spent searching for food.

Even so, there is still time for playing, socializing, and just hanging around. Chimpanzees are very social animals. They have preferences for friends and companions just as people do. They seem to express their emotions in much the way we do. There is a great deal of laughter and whimpering. They will touch one another to comfort or to tickle, or just to say hello.

Each group has a hierarchy in which certain chimps are subordinate to other chimps. The hierarchy may change as members of the group leave or die, or as a younger animal becomes stronger. Males are the dominant animals of the group.

A MOTHER AND YEAR-OLD BABY

The bond between mother and child is very strong. Chimps are dependent on their mothers for food, protection, and education. Taking a small chimp like Bruno was like taking a one- or two-year-old child away from his mother.

An adolescent female will help her mother with younger siblings. She will have her own first baby when she is about eleven years old. For about two years she will keep the infant close to her at all times. Even after that, the baby will play near his mother. The next baby will not be born until the first is weaned at about five years. The young chimp's emotional attachment to his mother is so strong that even when he is no longer nursing, a baby whose mother dies may

4

I have great sympathy for the great apes, even though I too have laughed at cute chimps dressed as human beings and performing tricks. Now that I have come to know chimps better, I am sad and angry when I see a chimp or any animal pay such a horrible price for my amusement. I take pleasure in seeing an animal as it is naturally; I do not enjoy seeing an animal forced to look and act like a person. I do not enjoy thinking of the dead mothers and the trail of dead babies that did not make it.

Bruno was the first chimp I knew personally. He made a great impression on me. He left New York to live with other chimps learning American Sign Language in Oklahoma. I went to college, but continued to look for ways to be with chimps.

After college I was asked to join a project that would take chimps out of the lab and bring them to an island. I jumped at the chance to work on it.

Because of this, I became privileged to know a group of eight chimpanzees very well, as well as—and maybe even better than—I know any humans outside my family. I want to share with you the admiration I developed by living side by side with them as they went from cage to freedom.

2 Inside the Laboratory

If a captured chimpanzee is a subject in a medical experiment, a laboratory becomes his home. There are several regional Primate Centers in the United States. Some have chimps. There are also chimps in some other labs. If a scientist or doctor wishes to do research with the great apes, he often rents an animal from one of these labs. The same animal is used again and again for experiments.

Many of the chimps are now born in labs. They are born to mothers who live in bare cages. There are no trees, no grass, and no wildlife around them to learn from, only cage bars and maybe a tire. They have no siblings, only their mothers and the sight and sound of chimps in other cages. In the first months they have no need for the rest of the world. Their little fingers cling to their mother's coarse black hair, and they suck on a warm, comforting nipple while the mother's stout fingers caress and groom the baby's body.

This bond usually comes to a harsh end when the infant is six months old. The mother is tranquilized and the screeching infant pried away from the unconscious adult. Without a nursing infant, the female will soon have another baby—yet another little chimpanzee can enter the world of the laboratory.

8

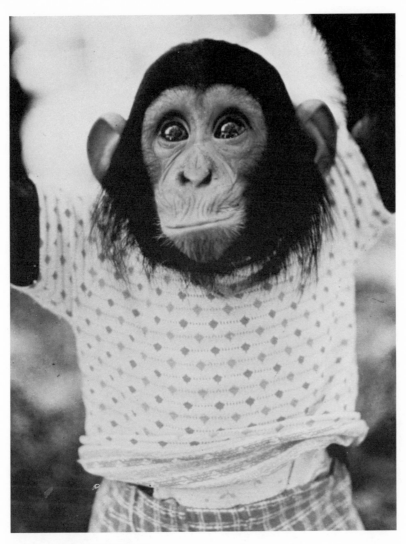

A DRESSED LAB CHIMP

The infant chimp may spend the next few months dressed in human clothes and nursing from a bottle. He becomes attached to a human being. By the time the baby begins to expect to be treated like a person, though, his life is changed again.

1000-MILE STARE IN A LAB CHIMP

What happens next is up to chance, largely determined by what experiments need chimpanzees. The baby is taken from being the center of attention and placed in a tiny cage. Often his chest is shaved and a number tattooed there. Many keepers feel that without a number they would not be able to tell the chimps apart.

The baby, who needs a mother and love, is left alone in a metal or plastic cage. When he is exhausted from screaming in fear, he may clutch the scrap of cloth some worker has put in with him, a poor substitute for a warm body. Often he cannot even see other chimpanzees, for the lab does not want germs to spread. Although there may be several young chimps in a room, barriers keep them from seeing or hearing one another. Some may spend the rest of their lives indoors alone in a metal cage. The smell of other chimps and disinfectant is strong in the windowless rooms.

In all fairness it must be said that captive chimps are usually healthier than wild chimps. They have fewer parasites and grow bigger. This is an argument scientists will use to help justify caged chimps. They have health, but no freedom.

The only excitement in the lab chimps' day is eating or participating in whatever experiment they are in. For animals who are used to a varied diet, lab food must be pretty dull. Plain monkey chow is their main diet. It contains everything they need to stay healthy. The chimps soften it with water they suck from a metal container. Some days a bit of fruit or vegetable makes the food more interesting. With so little exercise they tend to get heavy, so one day a week is a "starve" day. They are fed nothing at all.

Often this life wears at the chimps until many go mad. In order to pass the day they pace back and forth or sit and pick

11

LABORATORY TECHNICIAN AND CHIMP

at their hair—sometimes until they are bald. These behaviors are called cage stereotypies. Some chimps may become very timid, others wildly aggressive.

Each chimp deals with lab life in his or her particular crazy way.

Lab technicians are not intentionally cruel. A lab is a business, and that business uses animals. Scientists use chimps as subjects in experiments, just as they might use dogs, mice, or tissue cultures. They also want to protect their subjects. To be kept free from germs, animals must be caged separately and have their light, food, and excrement controlled. The people who handle them must wear protective clothing. Since many of the chimps are used in studies of human illness, the clothing also protects the people.

Because they are now so difficult to get, chimps are very expensive. This means that the medical people cannot use them in experiments that might kill them. They must try to use them in more than one experiment. The labs must also see to it that the chimps stay physically well, and, if possible, mentally healthy. Fortunately, labs are now trying to make life a bit more bearable for some of their chimps. The project I was involved with might help pave the way for some chimps to live out their lives away from a metal cage entirely.

At the time the proposal for the project was submitted, I knew nothing about the idea. I had just graduated from college and was in Oklahoma visiting Bruno. When I heard that two people were needed to work on a chimpanzee project, I flew back to New York immediately. My application was accepted, and suddenly I was part of the project. In New York also I met my co-worker, Tony Pfeiffer, who would soon become my husband.

13

Our project was funded by the National Science Foundation. It was designed to meet the United States government's need to find out if laboratory chimps could survive and breed on an island in a warm climate. If they could, their offspring would supply medical researchers with chimps that did not have to be captured in Africa. Two primate labs offered the project a total of ten chimpanzees. The Laboratory for Experimental Medicine and Surgery in Primates in New York offered facilities for housing the chimpanzees while they were being prepared for their new life on an island.

Once we had been assured of the funding and the chimps, we began to plan how to move the animals from the lab to an island in Mexico where we thought we could keep them alive, and where we hoped they might start to breed. From reading Jane Goodall's work about her life among wild chimpanzees in Africa, we had some idea what wild chimps are like. Her studies also showed us what we might hope our chimps could become.

Most of the chimps in our group had been born in the wild. We wondered if they remembered anything from their infancy in Africa. How would they deal with other wildlife? Would they get sick after years of isolation? Would they form a compatible group? There was so much about chimpanzees that we hoped to learn. We planned to keep careful records of daily changes in individual animals as well as in the group.

Whatever happened, Tony and I felt that for these chimps who were fated to spend their lives away from their natural habitat, life on an island in a semitropical environment would have to be better than life in a lab. We were not interested in breeding chimpanzees for labs. Still, someone would be doing a trial project to see if lab chimps could survive and breed on an island. We felt we could do it humanely and do it well.

But first, we had to collect the chimps and help them accept us and one another.

3 Meeting the Chimps

Hoots, barks, and pounding came from the deep woods behind the dirt road. It was an unlikely spot for a laboratory that housed two hundred chimpanzees and various kinds of monkeys. All of these African primates were strangely out of place among New York State's rolling hills. Yet in early June 1973 this is where Tony and I arrived to begin our lives with nine chimpanzees.

We had arranged to take chimpanzees who at the moment were free from use in medical research. We were to have nine chimps. Seven would come from this New York lab and two from another lab. The seven from the New York lab had been used in hepatitis research. We made sure they had no trace of this highly contagious disease and were otherwise healthy.

We wanted young chimps, eleven years old or less. Young animals, including humans, have an easier time than adults in learning things and adapting to new situations. These chimps would face a great change when we took them from a sterile lab to a semitropical island. We wanted them to have a fighting chance at survival. Hopefully, young animals would also show less cage-crazy behavior. They might also recall what it was like to be wild chimps. Finally, if the

THE INTERCONNECTED CAGES THAT HOUSED OUR CHIMPS

chimps fought as they came to know one another, young ones would not yet have large canine teeth. Among adult chimps, particularly males, the canine teeth are like daggers and can do a lot of damage in an instant's time.

It was impossible to get as many females as we wanted. Labs do not like to give up potential mothers. We settled for two females named Doll and Swing from the New York lab. We got five males—Cooper, Nolan, Spark, Dexter, and Alvin, from the same lab. The records showed that all of these animals had been born in the wild but had come to the lab before they were five years old. Two more chimps were still to join us.

Now we began to prepare the chimps we had for their island adventure. Before they were thrust into a strange and dangerous new world, we wanted them to get to know one another in the safety of the lab.

The lab gave us the use of a trailer in which we set up six large cages. Sliding doors separated each cage from the next, but the doors could be opened to form one large cage.

A heavy sheet of plastic ran under the entire row of cages. Urine and feces fell onto the plastic. Each day it was rolled up and burned in a special incinerator.

The trailer was kept at a constant 75° F. temperature, and the smell of disinfectant was worse than the chimpanzee smell. Fluorescent light glared off the white walls. It was not a pleasant place to spend six hours a day. But I planned to do just that.

"Our" chimps, as we came to call them, were brought from their small cages and placed in the big cages in the trailer. We left them in neighboring cages for a few weeks. This way they could become acquainted without being able to touch or hurt one another.

Ours was the first behavioral research work to be done at the lab. That is research that involves simply watching the animals and making notes but not interfering in any way. At first the lab technicians avoided me or were openly hostile. Then the day came when I helped pick up the plastic under the chimp cages. By the end of the day the word had quickly spread: "Linda did plastics!" By doing that messy job like everyone else, I became initiated into the lab.

Tony and I believed in doing all of our own work with the chimps. They were our responsibility. If we were really to know them, we had to clean up after them and feed them as well as do the scientific work. Chimps are tough and slow to show any sign of sickness. When they begin acting sick, it is often too late to save their lives. We had to get to know each chimp very well. We had to know if their appetites failed, if they did not play as much as usual, or if there were any other changes in how they usually behaved. These could be warning signals that they were ill.

Since Tony was working on his Ph.D. thesis, my job was to be with the chimpanzees. Every day I went to the lab. I sat against the wall opposite the cages, five feet away from the chimps. I wrote down everything that the chimps did and where every chimp was during every five-minute interval. This way we would know how the chimps were changing as well as whom they chose to spend time with. Watching them this closely hour after hour and day after day, I began to know them very well.

In addition to making behavioral notes, I fed them and handed out their vitamins. These moments gave me a chance to look everyone over and to try to touch or play with them. Some came immediately to be tickled or groomed through the bars. Others shrank to the back of the cage when

SPARK

20

I came in. Humans had captured, caged, and put them into painful experiments. It was no wonder they shied away or tried to bite me. I knew it would take time and much patience to get them to trust me.

Dexter, 110 pounds of solid muscle, was always distrustful. He would turn on me when I least suspected it. He'd thrust his finger out of the cage to touch me, and I would think how nice he was. Then he might give his finger a sharp turn so that his nail would rip my skin. He would seem to be so gentle as he took a vitamin from me with his lips. I would have to stay alert, for he might turn in a flash to try and nip me.

Spark was the first chimp to deal with me as an individual—as me, and not just as another technician in white. In the beginning he would crouch in the back of his cage whenever anyone came into the room. Nothing could coax him to the front to be touched or to play. I had decided to let him be. I could not force him to be friendly.

Then one day weeks later when all the chimps were together in one cage, I was passing out fruit. No one was letting Spark get any. I moved him into a separate cage. He became terrified. But when he realized that he was not going to his doom but rather getting to enjoy his apples in peace, his eyes seemed to say, "You did something for me, something kind." From that day on Spark and I were good friends. He came up to the front of the cage to play with me. Often he would turn his back to me, not to ignore me, but so that I could groom him. I had passed his test. I treated him as an individual and in turn he saw me as one.

After we introduced the chimps to one another in pairs and were sure they all got along, we left the doors open to form one long cage. Some of the chimps liked one another right away, others preferred to stay alone.

21

COOPER

Little Cooper and Nolan were friends immediately. Cooper, who had a flat face and almond-shaped eyes, was husky for a five-year-old youngster. He was outgoing and bold.

Nolan was a puny fellow with rotting teeth and a scrawny, bony bottom. He was five. Just before we got Nolan for the group he had gone through some nasty research in which a little bit of his liver was taken every week. During the last surgery he almost died. But spunky Nolan bounced back. He invented the trick of taking a sip of water, holding it

NOLAN

secretly in his mouth, and with careful aim showering the nearest human. He would then laugh with delight. His aim became so accurate that he was able to hit behind someone's eyeglasses.

Nolan was more hesitant than most in entering the big cage from his small isolation cage. He had lived in the small 2-by-3-by-4-foot cage alone since he was an infant. Going to the big cage took over an hour. Any attempts by me to force Nolan into the new space made him scream and sit rocking until he dared to try again. Bit by bit he did make it into

SWING

the big cage. He stretched out his arms and twirled until he fell laughing into a dizzy heap. Finally he hung on to the bars and did a few quick backflips. Seeing such joy in small freedoms I looked forward even more to the island.

Doll and Swing, both seven-year-old females, also got along well from the start. Swing was very dark in the face and had long, lanky legs. She was fearful and needed Doll. She would embrace Doll for comfort and reassurance. They often slept in each other's arms. Their friendship was so close that sometimes the bolder Doll would bring Swing a banana before one of the larger males got it. Doll was always very brave.

DOLL

Doll was also very clever. She was stocky with extremely bowed legs and a heavy brow ridge, which shaded her soulful eyes. Doll was quick to learn how to put on gloves, open locks, and even how to open the doors from the cage to the trailer. One day I was out of the room on the phone to Tony. When I returned, Doll was outside the cage in the room and there were new scribbles on my note pad. She had been imitating what she saw from the cage every day as I took notes.

Dexter was definitely the dominant male. He was older than the others and more forceful in his personality. He and Alvin played together quite a bit. A slap or a tight-lipped

ALVIN

glare from Dexter often reminded the easygoing, freckle-faced Alvin who was boss.

Everyone had a companion. Only Spark had a hard time fitting in. He was too old to be a play companion for Cooper and Nolan and too young to be taken seriously by Dexter. He spent much time alone, trying to keep peace with Dexter or picking on the little ones.

After several weeks, Tony and I felt that these chimps were accustomed to one another and would not be fighting dangerously. We set off to pick up the two other chimps that had been offered to us. We rented a truck and drove three hundred miles to another research lab. These chimps had been in cancer research. When they failed to get cancer and the project funding ran out, they could no longer be kept by the researchers.

JANET

Two tranquilized apes were brought out to us. Tony noticed that the female was not the one he had asked for. This one had plucked out all of her hair from boredom. The mix-up came as a great surprise to the lab technician, who said, "They all look alike." At least he knew males from females.

Soon we left with the two we wanted, Janet and Larry. They had all their hair, but we had yet to find out the terrible price they had paid for their years in solitary confinement. I had thought that the cage situation in the other lab was sad. There the chimps were alone in small cages, but they could climb the bars and see and hear other chimps. Janet and Larry had lived for years in smooth-sided, dark boxes. They could barely move, and certainly could not see other chimps. They had withdrawn into themselves and become

27

LARRY

really psychotic, not just neurotic, like the chimps we already had.

As we drove into the night, we heard only the mournful "hoo" from Larry as he staggered about dazed from the tranquilizer. When we arrived at our lab, we put Janet and Larry into large cages away from the other animals. We had to be certain they carried no diseases.

Like Nolan, Janet took hours of coaxing and prodding to get into her new cage. Unlike Nolan, once inside there was no joy for Janet, only aimless circling and repetition of a habit we called "tongue popping." She would sit for hours pressing her tongue to the roof of her mouth and sharply releasing her tongue. This produced a popping noise. She looked moth-eaten, her lower lip hung loose, and her eyes were vacant. Years without exercise had left her barely able to walk.

Larry was bigger than Dexter and had heavy bags under his eyes. He looked as if he had a crew cut. He was about eleven years old and had been born in the lab. It had been his only life. In a cage across from Janet he circled and ate. We soon discovered that Larry would much rather eat than do anything. His personal crazy behavior was to sit and wiggle his stubby fingers in front of his face. His fingers had become oversized and calloused from years of banging his fists against metal. He continued this with us, working the racket into a rhythm. He kept at it endlessly.

Janet had a serious problem. She would not drink from her feeder. In her old lab, she had only to put her lips to the nozzle and the water would flow. Here she had to suck. Sucking is a baby's first instinct, but for Janet the years in confinement had made her lose even the basics of survival. For three weeks we had to show her where the water came from before she finally learned.

I spent hours with Janet and Larry, but during that time they never responded to me. Nor, when we put them together in Janet's cage, did they respond to each other.

After a few days together Larry finally touched Janet. He hit her to get her away from the feeder. She screamed and ran into a corner. It was aggressive, but at least they were interacting. Being a male and more outgoing by nature, he soon began to explore his environment. He even began to use his massive arms to lift himself up on the bars.

After six weeks the isolation period was over. The time had come to put Janet and Larry with the other chimps. We left them in separate cages but in the trailer so the others

29

could study them. We could take no chances. We did not know how the group would respond to two crazy apes.

We didn't have to worry. The day the doors were opened Larry clung to the top of the cage screaming and Janet huddled in a corner screeching. The other chimps were a bit startled, but ignored them. Janet and Larry took a long time exploring the big cage. Larry sampled all the feeders. Janet tried to stay by herself. But she was badgered by Dexter, who thought he had found a mate, and by Nolan, who thought maybe he had found a mother.

As the months went by, I sat in the room with them, taking note of the changes. I also busied myself learning some chimp medicine in case they got sick on the island. I learned about the best drugs for chimps, how to give shots, and how to take blood. Medically chimps are treated more like children than like other animals. A pediatrician rather than a veterinarian should be their doctor. Because they had lived in a germfree lab for so long, we wanted to be sure they were protected against illnesses in the outside world. We gave the chimps vaccines to prevent tetanus, smallpox, and polio.

By January the group was well adjusted. They were used to us, and all the animals were healthy and inoculated. Larry and Janet were at least able to move around better. Sometimes they even made contact with the other chimps. A visiting photographer discovered that if one blew air into Larry's open mouth he would sit down and stop his wild banging. There was a gentle side to Larry.

We began opening the door of the trailer to give them some idea of the outside. A glimpse of sky or a bird flying by brought on a symphony of excited "hoos" and barks.

As the snow began to fall, it was well past the time we

should be heading to Mexico. We had already outstayed our welcome in the lab, but permission to enter Mexico was constantly bungled. We spent eight months at the lab instead of the three we had planned. The lab needed the space. Three days before the day we had made plans to leave, no matter what, we heard that there was no possibility of getting the chimps to the Mexican island. Now we had only three days to find a place to take the chimps, or the lab would reclaim them. Then all of our work would be for nothing, and they might go back into a medical experiment. Their chance for freedom seemed forever gone.

4 Leaving the Lab

The next two days were spent in a swirl of phone calls. Our search for a place to take the chimps reached a fever pitch.

Through some amazing good luck, Tony found someone who knew that Lion Country Safari, a commercial wildlife preserve in West Palm Beach, Florida, had an unused island they would be willing to let us use. We were overjoyed. At least this would be a temporary home for the group.

Florida seemed like the perfect place. Its climate was semitropical, with the temperature in the 50-80-degree range and very humid, although the location was not as exotic or secluded as Mexico. But at least we did not have to abandon the project. Lion Country also had the advantage of having experience with chimpanzees on islands. They had twenty-five chimps already. Mostly these were animals no longer wanted in circuses or as pets. Few, if any, had come from labs. Lion Country was the only place that had successfully kept and bred chimps on islands for over six years. We were sure to need their help and advice along the way.

The very early hours of January 27, 1975, found Tony making last-minute arrangements. I was deciding which of our possessions we needed and hastily throwing them into boxes. By the afternoon, we had rented a 22-foot truck, which we drove to the lab to begin the long job of packing up the chimps.

We wanted to avoid tranquilizing the chimps for the journey. Shooting animals with a dart from a tranquilizer gun always upsets them and can be dangerous if the dart accidentally hits the stomach or eyes. Also we did not want the chimps to be afraid when they woke up in a small box on a noisy, moving truck.

We had to make the painful decision to leave Dexter behind. We were not sure what Lion Country Safari would be like and felt that we could not take chances with an animal as strong and as dominant as Dexter. Our better judgment also said to leave Larry. As we had known him during those months in the lab, he might very possibly tear us apart given the opportunity. But I felt there was something special about Larry, a questioning, befuddled look deep in his eyes. I insisted we take him. Tony argued strongly against it, stating all the risks. I knew all the danger such a powerful and crazy chimp could cause, but I still wanted Larry. Tony finally gave in. We had to tranquilize Larry, put him into a 3-foot-square metal cage, and move him onto the truck.

Although it was a long, frustrating task, we were able to lure the other chimps into the transport cages with fruit and slam the door behind them.

We felt that Cooper and Nolan would feel more at ease during the long trip if they had each other to hug, so we put them in one cage. The same was true of the good friends Doll and Swing.

After three long hours we had the five transport cages in the truck, along with chow, fruit, and containers of water. We locked our personal belongings into an empty cage. Just

LION COUNTRY SAFARI

34

in case the chimps broke out, our things would be somewhat safe. Exhausted already, we were only beginning our thirty-six-hour trip to Florida. Unable to explain to Dexter why we left him behind, I could not look him in the eye as I said a last good-bye to him. My only consolation was knowing that he would have the run of the big cage for a time until once again he became part of an experiment.

In a freezing rain we began our trip south with eight chimpanzees.

Luckily the trip was uneventful. We drove straight through, taking turns to sleep, moving along as quickly as an overloaded truck could move. We stopped only for gas and toilets.

Only an occasional "whoo" from very bewildered chimps broke the silence. Much to our relief, there was no banging or shrieking. At every stop we gave them fruit, water, and some comforting words.

The glow of dawn found us approaching the chimps' new home: Section 6 of Lion Country Safari. On this 75°F. January day the sky above us was blue. The landscape around us could well have been Africa. Like the rest of southern Florida, Section 6 was flat and sparsely covered in pine trees. What was truly impressive to someone a mere thirty-six hours out of New York City were the rhinos, hippos, the elegant giraffes, and the grazing zebras all around us.

Spread out in the hundred acres of Section 6 were several islands where chimpanzees lived. Chimps cannot swim, nor will most dare to set foot in the water, so an island is a perfect natural cage for these primates. The canals around the islands were fifteen feet wide. They were a barrier for the chimps, but they also also provided drinking water for all the wildlife in the section. One island was empty. It was a lush third of an acre. No grazing animals had lived on it for years, so the grass was thick and the tall pine trees plentiful. Although forty feet high, these trees gave little shade, so a concrete pipe 8 feet high and 15 feet long would give the chimps protection from the sun and the rain. We knew sunburn would be one of our greatest problems in the beginning.

Lion Country provided us with a boat, or what was left of a boat after the damage done to it by rhino horns and elephant feet. Later we learned to push off quickly. This way we could cross the fifteen feet of water before the boat filled and sank.

With the help of Lion Country wardens, we got the cages off the truck, ferried them across the canal, and lined them up on the island. We were ready for the release.

I returned to the shore, with the canal between me and the island. From there I could get a better overview of all the activity and record it properly. Tony was on the island ready to open the cages one by one. As I watched my heart pounded with anticipation and my palms were sweaty. At long last these chimpanzees would feel grass, not bars, under their feet.

What would the chimps do? Would they be afraid to come out of the cages? Would they turn on us? The laboratory had suggested that, once released, they would seek revenge for years of caging. Would Tony need the gun he held? What if one of them ran into the water?

Alvin, the first to be released, stepped gingerly onto the solid earth. He moved carefully. Doll burst forth. She rushed up a tree, then down to the water. She was exploring every inch of her new home, as though she had never left the wild. She and Alvin came to each other, hugging and screaming with excitement.

LARRY EMERGING FROM THE TRANSPORT CAGE

Larry, however, charged about, his hair erect. He displayed his strength by throwing rocks and sticks this way and that. Suddenly, all 150 pounds of him were aimed at Tony. It seemed that perhaps the lab people had been right. "Tony, look out!" I screamed. Tony aimed the gun at the charging Larry. At the sight of the gun Larry sat on his hands and screamed in fear. The grand bully turned baby.

Doll went to Larry and panted her reassurance. Larry then went to sit by a large chicken-wire enclosure that was on the island, staring at the world through the wire as though once again through a cage. A free chimp seeking revenge for his years in a cage proved to be just another bit of lab lore.

Most of the others explored very carefully. They stayed close to the cages. But Janet and Swing were so frightened that they did not even dare to leave the travel cages. They sat huddled in the doorways, although they seemed curious about the world their companions were exploring. The cage was dirty and cramped, but to them it was a safe place, a place they knew.

After hours of pleading and many attempts to lure them with fruit and cookies, we decided it was too dangerous to leave Janet and Swing in the hot metal boxes. After making it this far, we could not let them die of heatstroke.

One of Lion Country's wardens had once been a cowboy, and he wasn't called Deadeye Harold for nothing. He could shoot a running chimpanzee with a tranquilizer gun from fifty yards. That seemed the only answer. Calmly and carefully Harold took aim. A perfect shot. The dart landed in the fleshy part of the thigh, the ideal spot to hit a chimp. Swing let out a quick shout, pulled out the dart, and groomed the spot. Janet did not make a sound.

Within five minutes we had two very groggy chimps. Janet began to stagger about. She tottered dangerously close to the water. Tony had to push and herd her, careful not to be bitten. There is a great danger if a tranquilized chimp tumbles into water. We would have to stand by helplessly as we watched the chimp drown. Jumping in after him or her would mean that as the chimp thrashed about, the human

LARRY'S FIRST DAY ON THE ISLAND

would be pulled down and drowned also. Finally the tranquilizer took effect, and both chimps collapsed in unconscious heaps. We put them into the large chicken-wire cage. There they could stay cool but be safe from running into the water when the anesthetic wore off. They still needed the security of an enclosed space. At the same time they could see the other chimps, the only familiar things in all of this newness.

Finally I could stay away no longer, so against all advice I went over to the island. Although I had been observing and writing down all that went on, I wanted to see the chimps without a canal between us. As I stepped out of the boat onto the island, Alvin leapt down from the top of a box where he had been resting. Again, Tony pulled the gun. I stood still, afraid of Alvin's strength but somehow certain he meant me no harm. He came very close to me. His strong, musty odor surrounded me, and I felt the dense weight of his hand on my head. For a moment I waited, completely unsure what would happen.

Alvin began to groom my head, touching and inspecting my hair. He had never seen it before, since it had always been tucked inside the lab hairnet. The wardens urged me away, still as certain as the lab people had been that he would take revenge for all his years of captivity. I was afraid, but also quite sure that Alvin knew me for myself as I knew him as an individual. I briefly let my hand sink into the deep coarse hair of his back before I backed down into the water and pushed off the boat. From now on I would visit them, but the island was theirs. Unlike the lab, they would be in charge. We would feed them and intervene only when necessary. The rest was up to them.

The sun was setting as we left the island. Tony and I were confident that the chimps had successfully survived their

SPARK BEDDING DOWN

first day. They seemed to respect the water as a barrier, and everyone was very cautious about it. Doll and Alvin, who had dared to climb trees, had not fallen. We had been told that outside the lab and free on an island they would not recognize one another and would fight. This was obviously not true, as the hugs and chatter continued. As the day ended they all lay around the enclosure that held Janet and Swing. They prepared to spend their first night on solid ground.

As we stood on the opposite bank, we realized that we had made it. Cages were behind us. All those months in the lab had paid off. The first step had been taken, we had brought our friends safely to their island home. Tony and I hugged each other and wept.

5 The Chimps' Island Home

The first few weeks on the island went by at an exhausting but exciting pace. With the same wonder one feels when watching a baby discover the world, we watched the chimps rediscover the world outside their cages. Tony and I came to the island every day to see the chimps make it their home. They explored every tree and every rock.

Everyone, including Tony and me, suffered some degree of sunburn from the fierce Florida sun. I had never realized how pale lab chimpanzees are until our chimps began to get brown all over. Their tanned skin made their coats look thick and dense like those of African chimps. Alvin did not tan; he just got more freckles.

Our greatest concern now was how the chimps would use the canal. We wanted them to drink from it, but not to try to cross it and drown. The day of their release we had felt confident that they were being very cautious by the water. But we had heard stories of chimps who drowned after several days. Maybe our chimps had just been too busy with all the other new things to try the water.

On the second day we got our answer. Alvin saw us on the far shore preparing to bring food across in the boat. In his impulsive, hasty way he could not wait. He took a flying leap. I suppose he hoped to land on the shore beside us. His leap was pretty good, but not good enough. Splash! He landed right in the middle of the canal and thrashed about wildly.

After a moment's panic I burst out laughing. Fortunately, the canal was so shallow now in the dry part of the winter, that Alvin had landed only chest deep in water. That was bad enough for Alvin. He was hysterical with fear. Unsure how Alvin would react in his fright, Tony waded in. Alvin seemed to be grateful and let himself be led back to the island. He was shaken but not so badly that he couldn't wolf down his chow.

The scene impressed the other chimps, because for quite some time no one dared venture too close to the water. In fact, Alvin never again even got his fingers wet. When fish came up to shore to nibble at chow that had fallen into the water, Alvin took great delight in hitting at them, but he used a stick.

Everything that was happening around us was as exciting and mystifying to us as it was to the chimps.

Spring came, and the torrential rains began. The first few times the wind picked up and the skies let down oceans of rain, the chimps were very upset. In Africa, wild chimpanzees will simply sit in the rain. It is so forceful there that it's no use even to seek shelter. But after a while our chimps tried to escape the downpour. The first raindrops would send them running to get inside the concrete pipe, which we called the culvert. Only Larry would stay out, getting drenched. He hooted and displayed. His hair erect, he ran around the island throwing objects and banging on anything

ALVIN DISPLAYING AT THE RAIN

that might make a sound loud enough to impress the others, the heavens, and himself. Soaked to the skin and furious, he would charge about, chasing the others out of the culvert as though to have them share his misery. Thunder and lightning upset all of them.

Fortunately, there was little chance the chimps would get bored on the island. If not eating or resting, they could always observe the other wildlife. Off the island, there were tourists driving by to watch or the goings-on of rhinos, zebras, elephants, and hippos. On the island there were turtles to poke at, rodents and birds to chase, and insect life

ALVIN INVESTIGATING A TURTLE

to watch and to eat. Cooper and Nolan took great delight in chasing rats back into their holes. It became Swing's obsession to chase off the blackbirds who came to steal part of the monkey chow.

Doll and Alvin continued to be the great explorers. Doll

DOLL SWINGING FROM TREE TO TREE

was zipping up trees, looking at the world from a higher angle. She soon felt so comfortable up there that she began to leap from one tree to the next. There were two trees close to the water's edge, about seven feet apart. Doll found that she could make the one tree sway, leap at the right moment,

NOLAN WAITING FOR DOLL

and land safely on the neighboring tree. The roots of these trees were raised up off the sand, forming a cave in the bank of the shore. Nolan, who was spending more and more time with Doll, would sit and wait for her, protected under the roots.

NOLAN'S FIRST CLIMB

Here in the open we realized what a scruffy little fellow Nolan was. Yet he had an endless supply of energy. We could see that he really wanted to climb up the trees with Doll, but did not quite dare. He would hug the tree and try a foot or hand. If he slipped, he made it into a game. He would push off and do a flip, as he had done against the bars in his cage. Little by little he made his muscles learn to climb. Probably he had been too young to learn in Africa before his

JANET

capture. In six weeks he was up trees after Doll. Soon they were taking turns leaping back and forth from one tree to the next.

The chimps discovered that behind tree bark lived bugs that were good to eat. They also enjoyed licking the sap. But without its bark a tree dies, and a dead tree soon breaks. Within weeks the chimps had begun to turn their island into land that was just as bare as the other chimp islands. Doll and Nolan were responsible for most of the damage.

Cooper, like Nolan, was very slow to learn to climb and did not spend much time in the trees. Spark only chased others up the trees. Janet and Larry never climbed. In fact, Janet took weeks even to leave the chicken-wire enclosure.

For the first two weeks we had to feed and water Janet separately in the enclosure. She would not leave. There was no roof, but Janet would not climb the mesh to get out. In her psychotic existence she stayed wherever she was put.

After two weeks the enclosure was pretty dirty. We felt the time had come to get Janet out. Tony cut a hole in the side of the enclosure. We put her food and water outside and showed her where it was. She caught on, came out to get the food, but took it back inside. Janet was in a rut. Having been caged so long, this was her security. When Janet came out one day to get her food, Tony covered the hole with a board and Janet stayed out. Wherever she was, Janet stayed.

After watching Janet for several days, we realized she was not drinking from the canal. Janet, who had taken three weeks to learn to suck water in the lab, was now unable to find and use the millions of gallons of water filling the canal. Here we could not take the time to pour water into her mouth three or four times a day.

But it did occur to me that I could begin to teach her how to drink. I went over to her with a paper cup full of water and I dribbled it into her mouth. She was thirsty and followed me as I moved to the shore. Every few steps I gave her another tiny sip. Finally we reached the canal. Now how could I get her to bend down and drink from the canal? I showed her again and again where I was filling the cup. No go. Janet just did not make the connection. Then it dawned on me. I held the cup under the water, and Janet in her robotlike fashion continued to drink from the cup. When I moved the cup out of the way, she continued to drink from the canal. Crazy as it seems, this was how I managed to get Janet to drink from the canal. Later on, she would some-times drink from my cupped hand.

Gradually, she did begin to move about, and after a couple of months she would walk around the whole island. But she wandered like a ghost. She watched the others, but she did not interact. Cooper tried for a time to be reassured by Janet. She may have seemed like a mother or an older sister to him, but his attempt to embrace her fell flat. Janet did not respond. Even so we felt she was making progress. We were all beginning to feel that Lion Country was a good home.

6 Can This Be Larry?

L arry took a long time to begin to explore the island and to find his place in the group. It had
taken him three weeks to leave the side of the
chicken-wire cage. In this stimulating environment he was
beginning to shed some of his lab craziness. But only some;
Larry continued to be a very unusual chimpanzee. Because
he was so big and aggressive, the other chimps had great
respect for him. When Larry launched into one of his
unpredictable outbursts there would be much scattering
and pant-grunting, a sound chimps make to show they are
being submissive.

No one was ever sure what might cause Larry to go wild.
He could be sitting peacefully in the culvert, tapping a stick
on the concrete. He would tap and tap and tap until he
worked himself into a frenzy. The next thing we knew he was
pant-hooting and becoming more and more excited by the
great echo he created in the culvert. Then he would begin to
sway, rocking himself into still greater agitation until, with a
burst, he would storm out of the culvert, throwing sticks,
rocks, and chimpanzees out of his way.

These displays impressed the other chimps as well as us.
A more normal, political chimp who used these displays at

LARRY DISPLAYING

LARRY SITTING ON HIS HANDS AND SCREAMING

the right time in the right way would easily have become the dominant male. As it was, Larry was simply unpredictable. He was a bully when he should have been peaceful, and a screaming coward at other times.

Spark and Alvin were very impressed with his clout at first, but they quickly caught on. If the two of them were having a fight, Larry became the "monkey in the middle." Alvin would grab Larry and push him at Spark. Then Spark would use Larry's force and hurl him back to Alvin. Larry would allow himself to be thrown about, screaming all the while, thereby adding to the tension. Chimps rarely bite when they fight; that would be like using knives. Hitting is usually enough. Larry seemed to know this too and would hit out. The other chimps were very specific about whom they hit. Larry hit anything or anybody before he would run off screaming in fear to sit on his hands.

LARRY MOUTHING ALVIN

At other times Larry seemed very thoughtful. He would sit by the water's edge and suck in the grasses from the canal like spaghetti. He loved to groom himself, other chimps, and eventually us. Maybe he saw it as the one social act he could perform. But, like some crazy humans, he did it to excess. He would corner Alvin and begin to groom his back. Pick, pick, pick. He worked at one spot, scraping it with his index finger until Alvin could not stand it anymore. Alvin would quietly get up and turn away. Larry persisted. This would continue for half an hour or so—Alvin moving, Larry following. Finally the spot would be bloody. Alvin would show Larry his canine teeth as a warning. Larry was not too sharp about chimp communication and would continue to pick at Alvin. Finally, in frustration and, in all likelihood, pain, Alvin would have a tantrum. He would scream and jump about, sometimes even hitting out at Larry. Then

ALVIN SCREAMING IN FRUSTRATION

Larry would scream too, and once again chimp pandemonium would break out.

Larry had other peculiar habits too. He would suck his nipple or walk across the island, rubbing one foot against the other at every step. The really strange thing was that Cooper began to imitate Larry. Cooper idolized the older, bigger Larry. Unfortunately we soon had two crazy-acting chimps. Luckily Cooper eventually outgrew his crush and took the more sane and sullen Spark as his model.

It took us over two months before we dared touch Larry. We were very close to the others, even playing with Alvin. I

TONY'S FIRST CONTACT WITH LARRY

was always a bit leery because of Alvin's strength, but Tony would flip him about and tickle him until he chortled with delight.

Larry still seemed very unpredictable to us — in fact, once he had to be shot in the leg because a Lion Country warden thought if he did not stop his charge Larry would catch me. I did not think I was in danger because I was already in the canal, out of his reach. Larry was always charging about like that, but luckily he was very distractible. A stone or a bird would catch his eye and Larry would stop his display to look at it instead.

I am not sure how it happened, but one day Tony decided the time had come to make contact with Larry. Tony calmly approached Larry, patted his head, and took his hand. Larry

A BIPEDAL LARRY

LARRY PICKING AT MY BUTTONS

melted. It was as though he had been waiting to finally be treated like all the others. He allowed himself to be groomed. Then he began to follow Tony around, holding on to Tony's leg. The second Tony stopped, Larry would sit and begin wildly to groom his leg. As he had with Alvin, Larry would try to groom the same spot until it was bloody, but as humans we were not as patient as Alvin.

Larry became fascinated with buttons and worked feverishly to groom a button off Tony's shirt. I stood by marveling at the new Larry. Then, on all fours, he came over to me. All at once he stood up. He was as tall as I am and twice as broad. He began picking at my buttons. His fingers, still thick and calloused from cage banging, twitched on my shirt. He panted at a quick pace in his version of a chimp grooming sound.

I was terrified. I believed in Larry, but I certainly did not trust him. Thinking that the buttons fascinated him, I ripped them off, gave them to him, and started to move back into

59

LARRY AND DOLL EMBRACE

the canal. Larry just dropped the buttons and followed me, walking upright. Then I learned what I needed to know every day from then on. Larry would magically sit and relax if I patted his head and stuffed monkey chow into his mouth. It seemed to be only his great excitement in seeing me that made him come at me bipedally. He only looked as if he were going to mow me down.

In days to come I spent many happy hours with Larry's huge arm around my shoulders as I fed him pieces of chow. But on that first day with Larry I felt entirely at his mercy. I sat very still on the bank beside him. Then he moved behind me in a duck walk. He crouched there and began to groom the freckles on my back. He picked at them and lipped them with his silky soft lips. It was a marvelous feeling to be treated like this by a chimpanzee, but especially by crazy Larry.

Tony and I left the island a bit shaky that day, but elated by the satisfaction that even Larry had been reached. Apparently, given enough time and the right conditions, even the most severely abused lab chimp could come to trust his friends. Our relationship with him did not make him a more normal chimp but it was satisfying. Even he and Doll reached some sort of understanding. In the beginning she had teased him mercilessly. As time went on they were sometimes seen playing or even embracing. We were all coming to know one another in this new setting.

7 A Brush
with Disaster

As always, the chimps began to scream and food-bark with excitement when I drove into the section. Within seconds they all stopped what they were doing and ran around to the part of the island opposite to where I parked the car on the mainland. In his excitement, Larry began to display, with Cooper pant-grunting and bobbing before him in submission. Doll and Nolan hugged, joyful at the thought of the meal to come, Swing jumped up and down, shaking her head and flailing her arms. There was incredible chaos and exuberance as the main event of the day began.

But on that day, two and a half months after our arrival in Florida, something seemed different. It took me some time to pinpoint it. Meanwhile, I tossed oranges and grapefruit across the canal to the chimps. These choice pieces of citrus I picked up daily from an orange grove. It was fruit that had fallen from the juicer or the truck. No longer satisfactory for humans, it became a delicacy for the chimps. Throwing fruit was a perfect way to distract them. While they were busy eating the fruit, I could take the boat across and spread chow around the grass and rocks on the island. In this way I did not have chimps hanging on me while I put out their food. Nor

ALVIN HEADS FOR A QUIET PLACE TO EAT ORANGES

was Alvin interested in stealing the entire bucket of chow if he had an orange to eat.

I never tired of watching how skillfully the chimps peeled the fruit skins. They used their teeth like paring knives. Even carrots were first peeled. Later, when all the fruit was gone, they scavenged about picking up peels. These were chewed into a wadge, then played with like chewing gum. They pushed it out on their lower lip, handled it, and used it as a sponge to get water out of places where their lips could not go, like the crooks of trees.

Usually everyone ran about grabbing up as much as he could. Soon arms, mouths, and sometimes even feet were full of oranges. Doll and Swing would always grab what they could and race up a tree to eat in peace away from the gluttonous males. Sometimes terrible fights would break out over one orange.

Cooper and Nolan would always hang back, afraid that the older males, Alvin or Spark, would hit them. Nolan soon learned that I carried fruit behind my back until I had walked to a safe spot away from the others. Then, as quickly as could be, I would toss it across the canal, and he would grab it and run to his favorite place under the roots of Doll's tree.

Today, as they all sat about munching on their fruit, it finally became clear to me what was different. Nolan was nowhere to be seen.

Just then he staggered out of the culvert. He took a few steps, then fell. He lay quietly, staring into the distance. My heart pounded. What was wrong? Again he got up, inched his way back to the culvert and collapsed. I jumped into the boat and pushed off to the island.

Quickly I rushed to the culvert, my mind racing through

the possibilities. A wound? A snake bite? What possible illness? I came up to Nolan, but he lay still. Was he dead? A crushing panic filled me. Then I saw trails of bloody diarrhea. How could he be so sick today and have shown no sign of illness yesterday? I was soon to learn that that was the way of chimpanzees.

Nolan was breathing, but I knew something had to be done without delay. He needed liquids or he would die of dehydration. I brought him some water, but he did not lift his head. I ran back to the boat, crossed to the car, and drove like a maniac to the main office. I called the vet, who said he would come immediately. I bought a Coke and got some Kaopectate from the infirmary.

Back on the island, I offered Nolan the special treat of Coke, a drink a chimp would usually fight for. Nolan did not even turn his head. I was desperate. "Nolan, please, please don't be so sick," I pleaded. Of course the other chimps were fascinated. Alvin finally came up and grabbed the cup from my hand. He raced around the island with it, slurping and spilling, five other chimps at his heels. Moments later Cooper was lipping Coke off the ground. The styrofoam cup was scattered all about, each chimp wadging a bit to get the sweet taste.

I sat with Nolan. His skin was dry and tight from dehydration. Tony, Dr. Sutton, the vet, and Harold drove up. We had to get Nolan off the island. There was no hope of treating him with the others hanging around. Harold got ready to shoot him with a tranquilizer gun. That seemed so brutal to me. I suggested that I try to inject him. The worst that could happen was that I would fail or that he would bite me. Then we would have to dart him after all.

Tony brought me a syringe of sedative. He kept the other

65

chimps away while I sat by Nolan. I talked quietly to him and showed him the needle. I did not want to take him by surprise. Weak as he was, he lay still. I patted his thigh and inserted the needle. Nolan only looked. When I pushed the sedative into his muscle, he didn't even flinch. I continued to talk to him and stroke him until he lost consciousness.

Tony and I carried Nolan to the boat, trying all the while to keep Doll from pulling his legs. Once on land we rushed him to the animal hospital. The first order of business was to get fluids back into him. Since he would not drink, we had to use intravenous feeding. Dr. Sutton inserted the needle into a vein and the glucose dripped into his body. The sedative should have lasted ten to twenty minutes, but an hour and a half later he was still out. It was clear that Nolan was very close to death.

The poor little body, the baby. He lay so still. After taking stool samples, Dr. Sutton found that the cause of the diarrhea was bacterial. We had become so cocky. The lab had warned us that the first two months would be a critical time for bacterial infections. Here we were into the third month and bacteria were killing Nolan.

When Lion Country chimps had picked up the same bacteria from the canal water, a certain antibiotic had worked. We treated Nolan with it and hoped it was not too late. I blamed myself for not seeing any signs of illness earlier. Now we could only wait. We settled Nolan in an isolation area off in the woods. He slept in his cage while the antibiotic and the bacteria waged war.

Feeling very sad and listless, I went back to watch the remaining chimps. It was getting to be evening. A nice time at Lion Country. No more tourists. The evening sun shone

A SICK DOLL

golden on the wildlife as they began to settle for the night in their private world without humans.

The other chimps were lying around enjoying the evening stillness. It seemed empty without Nolan skipping about on the shore. I had a few extra oranges, so I threw them as an evening snack. I felt ill as I saw that Doll stayed down, lying quietly. It was a nightmare. Even before going over on the island I went to get Coke and medicine. Perhaps she was not too ill yet and we could treat her on the island.

Doll did come over to greet me. She only took a tiny sip of the antibiotic mixed with Coke. She just wanted to lie on my lap. This was very flattering. At any other time I would have enjoyed it, but today I had to keep Doll from dying.

I got Harold, who tried to dart her with medicine. Everything went wrong. She was still strong enough to run when afraid, and run she did. When Harold finally did get a shot fired, the needle bounced off her tough skin. Then the dart broke. Maybe a bit of medicine entered her. We could only hope.

Tony and I decided to stay out to watch the chimps that night. At about 11:00 P.M. it became clear that Doll was getting worse. In the dark, with only a half-moon shining, we went onto the island. The stillness of the preserve was uncanny.

The boat glided across the still water. Even the scrunch of the sand as the boat landed sounded astonishingly loud. It was so dark that we had left the car lights on in order to see even shadows. I felt tense and breathless as I went to find Doll. We heard an occasional "whoo" as a chimp woke up. Without warning, Larry lumbered out of the culvert. He was walking bipedally. In the dark I could not make out the expression on his face, so I retreated into the water. Larry must have been just as startled, for he went back into the culvert and sat down.

Doll was lying on her side on the bank. I went up to her, saying her name so as not to frighten her. She looked up at me as I sat down beside her. I offered her some orange drink, but she just lay still. Those soft, soulful eyes would not leave me. All at once she got up and climbed on my lap. She wrapped her arms around my neck and put her head on my shoulder. I was utterly amazed. Doll clung to me. Her chest against mine was scorching. She was burning with fever.

We knew then that we had to take her off the island. "Try carrying her to the boat," Tony said. Certain that she would jump down if I moved, I got up slowly. I could not move very fast with the sixty pounds of Doll hanging on me. Slowly I began to walk down the bank. Doll did not move. "Get her into the boat," said Tony. I seemed to have no choice, but I was worried that she might change her mind and bolt once we were halfway across the canal. Carefully I climbed into the boat, my thighs tight and aching with the strain.

When Doll and I had sat down, Tony gave the boat a great shove and we glided across without a problem. We had no cage and no Lion Country trucks, so Tony said, "Get into the car with her." At this point I was just following orders. In the back of my mind I had some stray thoughts about a wild chimp running away in the dark of night, and all the trouble she could get into in a wildlife preserve. I also thought briefly about the danger of being in the back seat of a moving car with Doll, perhaps being bitten to death by a panicked chimpanzee.

All those thoughts were only far back, however. It was so clear that Doll trusted me. She needed me. She had given herself over entirely to me. I must in turn trust her completely. She did not flinch when the car started up or as we drove through the preserve. She just hung on to me. I realized I had never felt so close to another being, had never felt so needed. It was an overwhelming experience.

When the car stopped we were out by Nolan's cage. Tony opened the car door and asked, "Are you okay?" I just nodded. I walked carefully to the cage. In all the excitement over Doll I had not had time to think about Nolan. Would he be alive?

Alive he was. Even sitting up. Doll grunted, and Nolan jumped up. I hardly had the cage door open when Doll went leaping in to join Nolan. The two embraced. It must have been a great relief to them that they had each other, and that we had not taken them off to a laboratory or to total isolation.

It was easy to medicate Doll in her weakened condition. By the time we felt we had done all we could for the chimps it was 2:00 A.M. They were resting in each other's arms as Tony and I went to get some sleep.

Later that morning we went back to the cage not knowing what we would find. Much to our relief both chimps

NOLAN SITTING UP AS DOLL JOINS HIM

were alive. They seemed happy to see us but refused food or liquids. I spent a good deal of each day concocting goodies that the chimps might eat and persuading them to try. Some of the delights were rice and yogurt and Pablum with Jell-O. After they began to take some food, we could hide medicine in it.

Until they would take the medicine-laced food, it was necessary to inject them twice a day. At first we had Lion Country wardens try it. The chimps would scream and rock the cage, always ducking the needle. Often the humans holding the cage would be scratched or bitten. Doll and

Nolan created so much commotion that it was impossible to keep the needle in long enough for the medicine to enter.

I hated to see them carry on so, but without the injections they would not get well. I insisted that I try. I showed them the syringe. As they watched, I was able to inject the entire dose of medicine. I was amazed. It was then that I realized that chimpanzees must have a much higher pain threshold than humans do (that it takes more pain until they feel it). Therefore, most of the fuss was from fear. Doll and Nolan trusted me, so they did not need to be afraid. Instead they sat quietly for the shot.

A few days later I was cleaning the cage. I had to open the door a crack to do that. Doll was feeling much better, and before I knew it she had pushed the door wide open and was out and up a huge pine tree. And there we were in the middle of the woods far from everyone and everything! I began to plead. "Doll, please come down. What will I do if you leap off into the woods? Doll, there are snakes out there and the canals are full of alligators." Doll looked at me and looked at the woods. I am sure she was afraid too. Not of the snakes and alligators, for she did not know what I was saying, but she was afraid of the unknown. She knew me. Even the cage had familiarity to offer. After some minutes she made her choice. She jumped down into my arms and allowed me to put her back into the cage. Now I knew for certain that I had her trust.

There the two chimps stayed for ten days, until the bacteria had been conquered. Finally they were well again, eating and playing normally and eager to be out of the cage. We could return them to their island. We put the cage onto the boat, the door unlocked. There was always the awful fear that a cage might fall into the water with the chimp trapped inside. Tony walked the boat across. A good thing he is 6 feet 3. He kept the boat well balanced.

The chimps on the island were wildly excited to see Doll and Nolan again. Who knows what they thought had happened to them! Swing was screeching. Alvin and Spark were barking and came to sit on the shore. Larry, after displaying a bit, just sat and looked puzzled, as did Janet. Tony kept the others away by pointing a gun at them until the boat was firmly up on the shore and the cage door was hooked open.

Doll came dashing out. First she pant-grunted and bobbed at Alvin, the dominant male. Then she ran all over the island, up and down, checking out everything. As she explored she had a trail of chimps behind her. In the next minutes they all touched or were touched and hugged by Doll. There was no question that this was a warm welcome. She stretched out in the culvert, surely enjoying solid ground and freedom again. Alvin and Spark sat and groomed her.

Meanwhile Nolan timidly sat still in the cage. He seemed very afraid. Doll remembered and went down to him. She gave him a reassuring embrace, then left, as though enticing him to follow. She jumped about and flung sand at him, as if to say, "Come on, it's fun out here." It was very clear that she was really working at getting Nolan to join the group. It was also clear that he wanted to, but was frightened.

Suddenly Doll saw the light. She ran over to Alvin. She hopped about in front of him, playing him down to the cage. He swaggered in front of Nolan's cage and banged on it. Nolan shrieked in fear, then turned and presented his back side to Alvin. Alvin patted Nolan's rump. There it was: Doll had found the answer. As soon as Alvin had touched Nolan and reassured him that even though Alvin was boss he was

ALVIN REASSURING THE RETURNING NOLAN

happy to have him back, Nolan went running out of the cage. He jumped all over the island. He did twirls and hops. Then, much to our amazement, he stood in the middle of the island and did backflips. We burst into laughter. We were relieved and excited that this near disaster had ended so happily.

8 Janet

Our first run-in with trouble had gone so well that we were filled with new enthusiasm and confidence. The days sailed along. We established a good routine. We went out very early in the day to feed and observe the chimps. We collected information, data on the chimps' behavior exactly as we had in the lab, so that we could judge how they were adjusting or changing.

In the middle of the hot Florida days, the chimps just wanted to lie around. After a few weeks of sizzling our brains while watching the chimps sleep in the cool culvert, we caught on. We took a long lunch in an air-conditioned restaurant. Then we spent a few more hours observing as the chimps became active again in the afternoon. We left them with a second feed to last until morning. Since our chimps could not forage all day like wild chimps, we felt that two smaller feedings would be better than one large one.

Chimps and humans were doing very well until the morning of April 2. As usual, I went to feed. I had a habit of counting chimps as I drove through the preserve toward the island. No matter how often I counted, I kept coming up with seven. I panicked. I feared another sickness. It was Janet. Crazy Janet was not to be seen.

LINDA HELPING JANET TO A DRINK

I zoomed over to the island. She was not in the culvert, not lying along the shore. I could not find her anywhere. A chimp of Janet's size could hardly hide under a rock or behind the few pine needles on the trees. I searched and searched. Then I let the reality sink in. Janet was not on the island. She had not walked off. Not crazy Janet. She must have drowned. Janet was dead. For the moment all I could do was cry.

Doll came over to me as I sat silently on the shore. She looked at me intently for several minutes. She moved closer, pouted out her delicate lips, and tasted my tears. Her closeness and concern brought me around. I hugged her while Nolan began pulling on my shoelaces. I lunged around, yelling at him to quit it. How could he be so playful when

ALVIN INDICATING WHERE JANET WAS

Janet was gone? Of course he did not know or care the way I, a human being, did, but I was very bitter.

Tony came out and I told him. We began to search for where the body might be. We walked around and around the island. But we could see nothing, not even a spot where the canal grass was disturbed. We must have walked around for an hour, probing the water with sticks. No trace. Our frustration was almost replacing our sorrow. Then we noticed. Alvin had not moved. He sat by the rocks on the left side of the island. Tony went over to him. I stayed on the opposite bank. We looked carefully, and, sure enough, we saw where the grass was disturbed. Alvin had shown us the spot.

Tony had the grisly task of wading into the canal. He had to search for some time in the dark, grass-entangled water,

A WADING HIPPO SHOWING HIS TEETH

but then he found her. Tony struggled to bring Janet, heavy from her watery death, to rest on the sand.

Then the true horror struck us. Janet had not died by drowning. There was a huge, gaping hole through her chest and heart. Her death had been quick and violent. Our first reaction was that the fourteen-foot alligator that menaced the canals had clamped his jaws on her and dragged her down beneath the water.

We had Dr. Sutton come out and perform an autopsy. The results were shocking. It seemed that Janet's chest had been crushed as though by a steam roller. The force of the jaws that had clamped down on her was so great that her organs had burst inside her. The hole piercing her chest went through her body. Only one animal at Lion Country could have done such damage. A hippopotamus.

When the hippos came on the island to eat the chimps' chow, all the chimps would make certain to run out of their way. After years of caging, Janet's muscles could hardly get her to walk. Janet must have committed the greatest sin against a hippo; she got between it and the water. What was a simple chomp to that irritated hippo was for us the loss of poor crazy Janet.

She had just begun to make progress, to become a real chimpanzee, not a laboratory reject. We would miss her, but mostly we would miss not knowing how normal she might have become. We buried her in Lion Country sand. The chimps had made it safely out of the lab, but bacteria and the roaming wildlife made it a daily struggle for them to survive.

9 Alvin's Island

Life for the other chimps went on. They showed no signs of missing Janet. Of course she had never really been a part of the group. After a time of mourning for her, Tony and I resumed our routine. As the summer's heat thickened, the chimps' pace slowed down. The experience was not so new anymore, and they began to really use their environment. We were getting to know them better every day.

When a new behavior pattern appeared in the group, the little ones usually discovered it first in play. Perhaps rock throwing began as a result of Nolan's sitting by the shore and tossing pebbles into the canal by the hour. He and the others began to use bigger rocks and sticks, and in the hands of Spark and Alvin the rocks and sticks became weapons.

One day a photographer was with us. He wanted to film rock throwing. Alvin had begun to bombard any stranger, animal or human, who approached the island. It was no problem getting him to throw for the camera. I stood next to the photographer as he filmed. All at once Alvin scooped up a huge rock, using both hands to give it a good underhand swing. It was too late to turn, it was coming right at me. I felt a crack, then saw darkness as I fell under the water. I

ALVIN AND LARRY BOTH READY TO THROW ROCKS

ALVIN DISPLAYING WITH A STICK

80

scrambled to my feet. The wind was knocked out of me. Where the rock had hit hurt terribly. Alvin had broken one of my ribs.

Tony acted on impulse and sped over to the island, cursing and yelling at Alvin. If course Alvin had not hurt me intentionally, and even if he had he was just being a chimpanzee. Larry, as though to bring Tony to his senses, reached out his huge arm as Tony was running by. Splash. Tony's temper was cooled by a dunking into the canal.

As the chimps became more accustomed to their home, they became more territorial. Depending on their mood, they sometimes treated us as unwanted guests on the island. I felt the chimps thought of Tony as the dominant male, but of me as Wendy in *Peter Pan*, looking out for the lost boys.

Alvin's confidence was steadily building. One day as I was on the island feeding, Alvin stood by the shore and displayed. He began to pound on the boat and kick it, sending it out to the middle of the canal. I did not enjoy swimming in the same canal as hippos, so the next time Alvin began to display I threw sand at him. He became enraged. Not only did he continue to pound the boat but also to throw sticks and stones.

After two weeks of his nonsense I decided one of us would have to win this ongoing battle, and the one was me. Alvin began his display. He threw a rock. I threw sand. He worked himself up into another pant-hoot and threw a bucket as he backed me into the canal. I filled the bucket with water, ran back up the shore, and slushed it at him. We must have looked like two maniacs covered in sand and water, screaming and throwing things.

It got to the point where Alvin had run out of rocks around him. That did not stop him. He went to the other side of the

ALVIN CHARGING ME ON THE SHORE

island and collected more. I waited, ready with a pail of water. Every time he ran at me I drenched him. We kept this up for a half hour. I was trembling with rage and fatigue, but I knew I could not bow out then. At some point Alvin got sick of the whole thing—because, although wet he certainly was not tired. He ambled over to the culvert, food-barking on the way, and ate his chow. It was as if nothing had happened, except that he never bothered me about going on the island again. I went home to bed.

10 Tool Use

At the end of the first year on the island we celebrated what we called the chimps' rebirthday. I had made two banana cakes. One was for Alvin alone, and one was for everyone else to share. Sure enough, Alvin grabbed a cake out of my hand and carried it bipedally all the way to the culvert to gobble down by himself.

It had been a good year. Even though we had lost Janet, the other chimps were maturing and moving away from their laboratory selves.

As the chimps became more independent, Tony and I were spending less time with them playing or grooming. We still spent hours just sitting unnoticed and accepted on the island. To treat us like a rock was perhaps their greatest compliment to us.

It was on a day when I was just watching that Spark caught my eye. He was very intent on something, but I was not quite sure what. I continued to watch very carefully. Suddenly it dawned on me, and I swelled with excitement. Could it really be happening? Spark was termiting, or in this case, "anting." This was the behavior that Jane Goodall had used to make scientific news that man was not the only toolmaking animal.

ALVIN CLAIMING "HIS" CAKE

84

Chimpanzees in the wild seek out the proper stick, not too brittle, not too flexible, to poke into termite holes. They strip and whittle the stick with their teeth and fingers until it is just right. Then they put it into the hole and shake it. This makes the termites furious and they grab on to the stick, which is just what the chimp wants. He carefully pulls out the stick and gobbles down the termites shish-kebab style. And here it was happening just that way on our island. The only difference was that there were no termites. Spark was using ants instead.

I waved my arms and shouted to Tony, who was on the other side of the section photographing a hippo-rhino fight. Certain that some new tragedy had befallen us, he came running over. He was delighted. This meant that Spark must have remembered this complicated behavior from his childhood in Africa, maybe only from having observed his mother in the wild. Now, given the materials and the opportunity, it all came back to him. He certainly had not had a chance to practice that skill during those five or six years in the lab.

Fortunately we had ample opportunity to observe and photograph this behavior. Spark was very dedicated. He spent hours stripping leaves off sticks, whittling them down, then carrying them to a stump or a cluster of rocks, the two places on the island where the ants lived. This preparation proved what foresight the chimps have—they can plan ahead.

Soon the other chimps began to "ant," that is, all except Swing and Larry. Alvin also seemed to be a real pro. Maybe he too remembered.

As usual, Doll was the most creative. She found the easy way. She made a tool, then simply turned over a rock until

SPARK CARRYING A STRIPPED STICK TO AN ANT SITE

. . . INSERTING THE STICK IN AN ANT HOLE

. . . LIPPING THE ANTS OFF THE STICK

HIPPOS GETTING THE CHIMPS' CHOW

she found swarming ants. She put the stick among them and they hung on, giving her a tasty treat. She didn't have to bother finding a tiny hole.

Nolan only fooled around, but Cooper worked very hard. After watching the older animals he got the idea of anting. But the stick he tried to poke into the tiny hole was much too thick. I had to admire his patience. The only time he seemed to get an ant was when he lipped one off the outside of the stump.

This behavior lasted as long as the ants did. At some point they seemed to be all gone. Still, from time to time someone would make a tool and try the stump, just in case an ant had returned. Finding no ants, they might use the stick to clean their teeth.

The chimps also used sticks against the hippos, who were becoming increasingly bold. We did everything we could think of to keep the hippos from getting the chow. We put it on top of the chicken-wire cage, in the middle of the culvert, and around the rocks. But minutes after we had spread it around they were up on the island scavenging. Needless to say we were very sensitive about hippos and the damage they could do.

Often Swing would let out a "whoo." She seemed to be the sentry. It took our eyes a while to spot the intruder, but sure enough either a snake, turtle, or just the eyes of the hippo would be visible in the canal. The chimps became very casual about most of the wildlife sharing Lion Country with them except the snakes and the hippos.

They seemed to be instinctively afraid of snakes. They kept their distance "whooing" and sometimes screaming in fear, except for Larry, who once picked up a snake and began to munch on it. Luckily it was a harmless black snake and not one of the poisonous cottonmouths that slithered around the preserve.

Sometimes if we spotted a hippo and started action while it was still in the water we could keep it from getting onto the island. If we began shouting, shooting a BB gun, or throwing rocks, we could sometimes get the chimps to do the same. Then the hippo seemed to feel that climbing on the island was not worth the chow. It would submerge and head off elsewhere. Only bubbles on the water's surface would tell us a 3,000-pound hippo was swimming by.

If the hippos made it onto the island, there was little we could do to be rid of them until they were ready to leave. The chimps armed with sticks and rocks did their best to seem fearsome. Spark and Alvin put on a very brave show, displaying from a distance. Alvin might sneak up quietly behind one of the younger animals, pull his tail, or slap his rump and quickly run away. The only response was a slightly annoyed look from the hippo.

If the hippos had had their fill, a group effort by the chimps often got them running into the canal. Then, with a great splash their huge bodies would disappear beneath the water. Spark and Alvin always took command of these at-

THREATENING THE HIPPOS

tacks. They would pant-hoot and throw their weapons.
Nolan and Cooper would run around practicing their pant-
hoots.

Doll was always very brave. She seemed to like to tease
the head end as well as the other end. I guess Doll just liked
to live dangerously. Larry would get caught up in the
excitement, but, in Larry fashion, he always came in too
late. Just as the hippo disappeared into the canal Larry
would come blustering down to the shore. His hair erect, he
sat bobbing his head, looking as though it were all his doing
that they were gone.

Eventually Doll and Nolan became so brave that they began to play around the hippos. Once we even found Nolan jumping from one hippo back to another, as though they were boulders. This was not very wise. One of Lion Country's chimps had been killed doing the same thing.

The hippos were just a part of Lion Country we all came to deal with in our own way.

11 Freezing in Florida

The second winter we spent in Florida was bitterly cold. Chimpanzees can stand some hours of low temperature at night, as long as they also have a chance to warm up during the day. The temperature would drop into the thirties at night and would not go above 50°F. in the day. It was very windy and raw, terrible weather for the chimps.

We were constantly worried that the chimps would get very sick. They can easily get respiratory infections. What to us would be a slight cold will quickly become pneumonia and death to a chimp. We gave them burlap bags and old clothing. Tony went on television to ask for old blankets. We did get some blankets donated, but the chimps pulled and ripped at them and tore them apart in games of tug-of-war. They did seem to know that wet blankets would not keep them warm. At least on the very cold days they were careful to keep them from falling into the canal. We did our best to pick the scraps out of the canal and let them dry. Yet slowly but surely the blanket supply was disappearing.

Instead of providing shelter, the concrete culvert just held the cold and acted like a wind tunnel. No matter how cold it got, the chimps would not huddle together for warmth. They liked to sleep alone.

ALVIN NESTING

In the morning, it was so cold that Tony and I could hardly get out of bed. We would arrive at the island to find the chimps ashen gray and shivering. Nolan's feet became so badly chapped that the skin was split and bleeding. As the sun began to rise, the chimps would each find a spot where the sun hit and where rocks and tree stumps kept the wind off a bit. There they gathered hay, sticks, and blanket scraps to make nests—all but Larry. We would drape a blanket over him, but he did not get the idea; he just kept walking until the blanket fell away. He was a creature of habit and continued to lie shivering in the culvert.

NOLAN INVESTIGATING THE FIRE

During the day we put out hay. But as soon as we were gone, the hippos would amble over to devour it. We tried leaving bales on the hippos' side of the canal, but the island hay seemed to taste sweeter. This left the chimps with no warmth for the icy-cold night.

We tried building fires on the island. As was to be expected, the chimps were frightened and kept their distance. They did sit against the concrete that had been warmed. Once the fire was out they would lie in the pits, which were still warm with ashes. Perhaps if we had made fires every day for months, they would have learned that warmth was worth the fear.

PLAYING ON THE BOXES

A generous family in Palm Beach came to our aid. Diana and Allen Manning bought some lumber for us. With the wood we built seven very strong 3-foot-square boxes. Each of the boxes had holes in the sides so that we could tie them together. When they were all assembled on the island, there was a tight circle of boxes, the entrances facing in—like a wagon train.

We hoped this design would allow each chimp his or her individual sleeping place but keep them grouped for protection against the cold and the hippos. It was no easy task getting the boxes set up on the island. Each box weighed a hundred pounds. As always, the chimps were very curious, and it took the sight of a BB gun to keep them away. At one point as I was hammering a loose nail into place, Doll jumped onto the box and began to imitate my hammering with a rock. It never ceased to amaze me how clever she was.

One night in mid-February the box beds were ready to be tested. We hoped for the best, since the weatherman predicted the temperature would drop into the twenties. Before we left that evening, we dumped two bales of hay into the center of the boxes. Before we had driven out of the preserve we saw with delight that the chimps were already jumping into the boxes after the hay and staying in there. We were worried Larry would continue to shiver in the culvert. Much to my relief, as we were driving out of the gate, I saw Larry lumber up and into one of the boxes.

Tony and I had just sat down to a hot bowl of soup when the head warden of Lion Country phoned. He asked if we could please come out and help. It was getting so cold they needed to get some hay out to their chimps. They also needed to set up some space heaters for the elephants. Of all the exotic animals out there, the elephants suffered the most from the cold. They have so much surface area and no way to huddle.

We put on long underwear and drove back to the preserve. As we got to each of the other chimp islands, all we could see were mounds of dark shapes. It was so cold that they were lying on top of one another. Stiff with cold, they gratefully took the hay and piled it around themselves. There was no time for careful nesting. We did not know if this would be enough to keep them from freezing to death, but we had done what we could.

We approached our island and shone the car headlights on it.

For once it was with great relief that we did not see any chimpanzees. They were all tucked away inside their new boxes.

Judging by what we found the next morning they had been kept safe and warm. All the hay was still there. We found beautiful nests in each box. The boxes were hippo proof! From now on we could also put chow into and on top of the boxes.

Of course, as the weather warmed the boxes became great toys and display objects. Larry especially liked to bang and toss them about. No matter how many nails we put in them, or how often we rewired them, the boxes were thrown about. They survived only two winters. They had served their purpose and more. We kept the chow away from the hippos and no one even got a cold those two winters.

12 New Beginnings

As we moved into the third year, life was settling into a familiar pattern. Parasites and hippos had become part of daily life. The chimps knew and seemed to accept their days on the island as their life, their home. Just as the lab had once replaced their African lives, so now the island had replaced the lab. They clearly were not, could not be, like wild chimps. That ability had been taken from them forever the day their mothers were shot. Yet they were no longer like lab animals, victims of the humans who confined them.

In the process of change, perhaps like children growing up, the chimps did not need us as they once had. Compared to other humans, we were still very special to them. They relied on us for food, but otherwise they were interacting as a group of chimpanzees, not as individual singly caged animals.

It was curious that this odd mixture of chimpanzees—young lab animals, mostly males—could become such a close-knit group. Again, this was not what we had been led to believe possible. They certainly were not like any wild chimp group, but then certainly it was not an African environment. They were adjusting to the island, working

ALVIN, NOLAN, COOPER, AND LARRY

out their relationships, be it chasing hippos or just relaxing. As each chimp's personality grew and left more of the lab behind, so too were the group dynamics changing. Both as a group and as individuals our charges were becoming more independent.

As usual, Doll illustrated this new self-confidence best. Of all the chimps, she used the island to its greatest advantage. She loved to explore, and she had the confidence to experiment. Perhaps because she was so strong-willed, she was quite dominant in the group. Unlike most chimp females, she would fight back if Alvin hit her. We called her the first liberated female chimpanzee.

Nolan especially found Doll very appealing. Cooper bullied Nolan, and therefore was no fun to play with. Doll was a great playmate and good at giving hugs. She was a friend and a mother to Nolan, two things he very much needed. Since she enjoyed quite a high status, she would also protect baby Nolan from being pestered by Cooper and picked on by the big males.

In Africa chimps will go to great trouble to leap streams so that their toes don't get wet. Doll seemed to say, "This isn't Africa, it is Florida and I am very hot. Look at all this canal water." She began slowly to explore the limitations of the canal. Soon she was splashing around in the shallow shore, then backing carefully farther out beyond the roots. She always kept a careful hold on something solid until she was sure where her feet would land. Before long she was sitting out neck deep, cool and refreshed while the others sat hot and fly-covered in the culvert.

Nolan was not to be left behind and soon they were both splashing in the canal water. Nolan adored having a human splash water into his mouth. Dripping wet, he would roll again and again in the sand until he looked like a breaded cutlet. One of the best benefits of daring to enter the canal was that Doll and Nolan got all the oranges that fell there. They just waded out until they could grab them. But even for an orange they never went too far or too deep. They learned to cup the water with their hands to bring the fruit in closer. The greed for food did get Cooper out into water knee-deep, but no one else dared enter the canal.

Doll knew that the boat was the way to cross the canal. I had begun to tie it up with six knots while I fed the chimps, or she would have it untied and pushed off before I could turn around. It became a nightmare trying to keep Doll off

99

DOLL TRYING TO MAKE A GETAWAY

the boat. She did not like being crossed and would grab and pinch my leg if I tried to stop her.

Then Doll found another way to see the rest of the preserve. There was little or no rain during the winter, so by early spring the canal was low. I could stand chest-high in the middle. So could Doll. I had noticed that the sneakers I wore only on the island and left near the boat each night were scattered far and wide in the morning. At first I suspected a passing rhino or zebra. Then one day, as I sat on the

DOLL WADING ACROSS THE CANAL

preserve side taking data, I looked up to see Doll carefully making her way across the shallowest part of the canal. She picked up my shoes and carried them back across the canal above her head. No matter how much I begged and shouted, Doll ignored me and calmly put on one shoe and ripped the other apart.

I could not believe what had just happened. Unfortunately, I had plenty of opportunity to learn to believe it because Doll did it again and again. We came to the painful

NOLAN SCREECHING AT DOLL TO RETURN

conclusion that we would have to cage her elsewhere in the preserve until the rains came and raised the water level in the canal. There was too great a danger that she might be hurt by one of the other animals, hurt a tourist, or, worst of all, escape into the Florida woods.

After a couple of weeks we felt there had been enough rain to keep Doll on the island. She had been a well-behaved prisoner, and we had spoiled her with good things to eat. Of course, when we took her cage out to the island she began to scream with delight and excitement. Nolan stood chest-high in the canal, screeching, his arms reaching for Doll. It was the warmest of reunions. Unfortunately Nolan was not enough to keep Doll on the island. Next time she took him along. He was not tall enough to walk across, so Doll floated him across on her arm. This time they were imprisoned together.

102

SPARK AND ALVIN BATTLE AS COOPER EGGS THEM ON

The madness went on until the heavy summer rains came and filled the canal. But it began again the following year. Doll's escaping was bad enough, but we also worried about the added risk of bacteria in such sludgy water. Although it was a great expense, we decided to have the canal widened. What an event! Larry and Alvin were exhausted from displaying all day at the steam shovel.

The canals were now deep enough to keep Doll from walking off, but she went back to her old routine of stealing the boat. Compared to walking off, this seemed trivial. I did not like the solution, but I began to carry a BB gun to scare her away from the boat.

It was not only because of Doll that I had to carry a BB gun. Alvin and Spark were becoming tougher and stronger. They were young adult males. It had been fine to have three juvenile males living in such a small space, especially since

Larry did not act like a normal chimp of his age. But now that they were more mature, each wanted more space and more power. They were beginning to act like adults. Their fights were less frequent but more severe. They were getting some serious wounds. Alvin once had his lip ripped in half. Spark had a huge piece of his foot taken out by Alvin's mature canine teeth. Their fights were now the real thing.

The fights seemed to center around the females. They too, were becoming sexually mature, and both Spark and Alvin wanted them.

Doll remained very independent in these matters. She wanted nothing to do with the males sexually. Swing, on the other hand, changed dramatically. No longer a shy and fearful juvenile, she used her new power to become bold and pushy. She soon learned that the males would not hurt her or chase her away. As a result it was not unusual to see Swing take food right out of Alvin's mouth or to push Spark over for a shady spot in the culvert. I loved seeing her blossom.

She also became more outgoing with me. Instead of hanging back when I was on the island, she would come over, grab my leg, and shake her head around in circles to invite me to play. Swing was also incredibly tender. She loved to groom the salt from my eyes. Her fingertips were like velvet when she touched my eyelids.

Spark and Alvin had less and less contact with us. The BB gun really upset them. Doll only took it half seriously. She knew what a softy I was, but the big males did not take it as a joke. It seemed to mean that I should be watched out for. Their fear sometimes made them angry, and those were the times I needed the gun. They would become crotchety and strike out.

We were still friends. Sometimes Spark and Alvin played with us. But their strength was beginning to scare me. I no longer had any control, and I am sure they sensed that.

Alvin still liked to be tickled, but when he had enough he would try his old lab trick of ripping my skin with his finger nail. One day, as we were playing, I felt intense pain in my hand. I looked and blood was soaking the sand red. I stood amazed. So did Alvin. He came over and gingerly lipped the blood from the sand. I suppose he was surprised a play bite could draw blood. More likely he was just curious what the stuff was. My skin was just not as thick as a chimp's, so his canine had gone deep into my palm. This was clear proof that the chimps were becoming too adult to play with. They might not mean any harm, they were just too strong.

We always knew that they were chimpanzees, not pets. We were proud of our relationship. We felt that we were accepted by the chimps. They treated us like people and we treated them like chimps. Because there was mutual trust, we could interact on many levels, from friends playing to caretakers saving lives. People would sometimes ask us why we did not have a chimp at home. What Larry did to the boxes and what Alvin did to my hand were answer enough. A chimp is too complex an animal to be a pet.

Larry was the exception. He was always a step behind. We were spending more time with him as the others drifted away. He was now playing and acting like a chimp half his age, enjoying the childhood his cage had not allowed him to have. Cooper's former idol had become his playmate. And Larry was becoming more gentle all the time. Somehow I trusted him more than I trusted Cooper. Larry just wanted contact. He would sit by my side gently grooming, or he would just sit. To me he was now predictable. A gentle giant. He had needed a chance. I was so grateful it had been given to him.

Cooper was becoming the unpredictable adolescent who

LARRY AND LINDA

loved to test us. He was frightened of Tony, but he took great delight in punching me whenever he could.

As things changed with the chimps, they were also changing with Tony and me. We had had no money from the government for two years. We had been feeding and maintaining the group through the generosity of Lion Country, the Fund for Animals, the Humane Society of the United States, and from our own pockets. We had done everything we could to keep the project going. Much as we loved the chimps and the work, we felt it could no longer go on this way. When we did not get another government grant we had applied for, we had to make the painful decision to leave. The day the decision was made I sat on the shore and wept. Larry and Doll, curious as always, licked my tears.

October 25, 1977, was our last day at Lion Country. We had made arrangements that the chimps could stay there until the time when we had found them a permanent home. We would do everything we could to keep them out of the laboratory. Perhaps someday it would be possible for us to be with them again. Now we were heading back to New York without them.

It is hard to describe the ache I felt standing on the shore saying good-bye. We had shared four wonderful, growing years. There was some comfort in knowing the chimps did not need us the way they once had. We had done what we set out to do. These crazy lab chimps had survived three years on an island. They were tough now. They were chimpanzees, not shells.

I worried about Larry. Perhaps someone else feeding him might not know that a pat on the head, not a gun, would stop his insane displays. I told myself if something happened to the chimps now, at least they had known freedom for three years. I was proud of that.

But I was sorry we could not follow their development further. Who would be dominant male? Would Doll have a baby? Would Nolan ever lose his baby giggle? In fact, would he ever grow up? Hopefully, we would visit and find out for ourselves.

Of course they did not know it was our last day, only that everyone had been hugged and two watermelons passed around. I watched them eat. Tony urged me away. Before I turned to the car, I picked up my well-worn sneakers and

tossed them to Doll. She would have fun with them. I would not need them anymore. But before Doll could even turn from her food, Nolan had dashed over, scooped up the sneakers, and scrambled up the last standing tree. Even then, choking on tears, I had to giggle as Nolan bombarded Cooper with my shoes.

13 A Return Visit

The years passed quickly. The empty place the chimps had left began to fill up with a different life for me. New jobs, new cities, and a baby boy of my own occupied my time.

Instead of feeling tearful and worried every time I thought about the chimps, I found that they had become a solid part of my past. Like old friends, they were absent, but never far from my thoughts.

Then, in the summer of 1980, I had the opportunity to visit Lion Country Safari. With great excitement and anticipation I approached the chimps' island.

Would they remember me? Would they allow me onto the island? Would they be angry with me, or even in their excitement hurt me? I was most anxious to see if Doll and Swing had babies. That would really be the greatest proof of their successful adaptation to the island.

As I stepped from the car I knew I need not have worried about their remembering me. First Nolan, then the others, one by one, noticed me. They screamed and hugged each other in excitement. Nolan came halfway across the canal, held out his arms to me, and screamed. He still had the same baby face, but now on the hulking body of an adult. I was surprised at how intense my happiness was to see them again. They all looked so very healthy, so beautiful, so content. So grown up.

Alvin was the biggest chimp in the park now, certainly the dominant male on the island. Spark, handsome as ever, displayed and charged across the island. Swing seemed her gentle self. She sat on the shore, still long and lanky, bobbing her head at me. Doll clearly recognized me, but she sat up on the culvert, where I could not get a close look at her. She was panting and hugging everyone who jumped onto the culvert.

Cooper seemed to be even more of an outcast. He sat away from the group and rocked. He had never fit into the group in any sort of comfortable way. Larry, who had become his friend and companion by the time we left in 1977, was gone. He was dead. No one knew why. I sensed that the special unpredictability and warmth he gave the island were no longer there. I missed him.

As I traveled across the canal just as I had hundreds of times before, I felt as though I had never left. Apparently the chimps felt the same way. When I arrived on the island, Doll took my hand and walked me to the side. Now, so close to her, I could see, nestled against her chest, a very tiny, six-week-old baby chimp. I touched his velvety pink face. Now there was a new life, a baby born outside of the lab. As Doll allowed me to touch him I was determined that he would never know life surrounded by bars. I was overcome with emotion at the trust Doll showed me, an adult chimp letting a human she had not seen in three years so close to her baby.

110

DOLL AND HER BABY

Leaving again was not easy. But at least I knew that the chimps were well. Mutual trust and joint effort of both chimpanzee and man had combined to make a new life possible for them. They had gone from cages to a special kind of freedom.

Further Information on Chimp Rehabilitation Programs

The Humane Society of the United States
2100 L Street N. W.
Washington, D.C. 20037

Interagency Primate Steering Committee
N.I.H. Building 31, Room 4B30
Bethesda, Maryland

International Primate Protection League
P.O. Drawer X
Summerville, South Carolina 29483

Primate Foundation of Arizona
P.O. Box 86
Tempe, Arizona

University of Texas System Cancer Center
Science Park, Veterinary Division
Route 2, Box 151-B1
Bastrop, Texas 18602

Bibliography

Brewer, Stella. *The Chimps of Mount Asserik*. New York: Alfred A. Knopf, Inc., 1978.

Maple, Terry. *Chimpanzee Reproduction, Rearing and Rehabilitation in Captivity*. Report presented to The Ad Hoc Task Force Natural Chimp Breeding Program, Tanglewood, North Carolina. Atlanta: Georgia Institute of Technology, School of Psychology, 1980.

Teleki, Geza, Karen Steffy, and Lori Baldwin. *Leakey the Elder: A Chimpanzee and His Community*. New York: E.P. Dutton, 1980.

Teleki, Geza, and Karen Steffy. *Goblin, A Wild Chimpanzee*. New York: E.P. Dutton, 1977.

Van Lawick-Goodall, Jane. *My Friends the Wild Chimpanzees*. Washington, D.C.: National Geographic Society, 1967.

INDEX

ABOUT THE AUTHOR

Linda Koebner grew up in a house full of animals. She first developed a special affection for chimpanzees when she met Bruno, a young chimp learning American Sign Language. She has worked in the Department of Animal Behavior at the American Museum of Natural History and at Cambridge University, Cambridge, England, and has done field work with Vervet monkeys. *From Cage to Freedom* is her first book. Her reunion in Florida with the chimpanzees, described in the book, was filmed and aired on the television show *Those Amazing Animals*. Ms. Koebner and her young son live in Mount Vernon, New York.